Ladybird Readers

The Picnic

W0009173

Based on the Learning Time with Timmy TV series
created in partnership with the British Council

Watch the original episode "Picnic Time" online.

995146654 0

Picture words

Timmy

Osbourne

Stripey

Otus

Bumpy

picnic

carrot

sandwiches

Timmy and his friends are happy. They have a picnic.

They go to the garden.

Osbourne has a book.

Osbourne opens the book.
What can you see, Stripey?

Stripey can see a carrot!
Stripey loves carrots.

What can you see, Otus?

Otus can see a banana.
Otus loves bananas.

What can you see, Bumpy?

Bumpy can see an apple.
Bumpy loves apples.

Yes! Carrots, bananas, and apples are in the picnic!

What can Timmy's friends see on this page?

Sandwiches!
There are sandwiches in the picnic, too.

Timmy is happy.
He loves sandwiches!

Your turn!

1 **Talk with a friend.** 💬

What is in the picnic?

There are apples and sandwiches.

What does Bumpy love?

Bumpy loves apples.

2 **What color? Listen. Circle the words.**

1  red ⟨green⟩

2  orange yellow

3  yellow red

4 blue green

3 Listen and read. Match. 🎧 📖

1 I love carrots!

2 I love bananas!

3 I love apples!

4 I love sandwiches!

4 Listen. Write the first letters.

1  carrot

2  banana

3   apple

5 Sing the song.

What is in the picnic? It is a carrot.
I love carrots!
What is in the picnic? It is an apple.
I love apples!

Timmy and his friends go to the garden.
Timmy and his friends have a picnic.
I love, I love picnics!

What is in the picnic? It is a banana.
I love bananas!
What is in the picnic? Sandwiches.
I love sandwiches!